For Mum and Dad
- D.C.

For Matthew, Ben and Rachael
- B.O'D.

For Nicholas
- B.E.

Special thanks to Caolán and Murphy

First published in Ireland by Discovery Publications, Brookfield Business Centre,
333 Crumlin Road, Belfast BT14 7EA
Telephone: 028 9049 2410
Email address: declan.carville@ntlworld.com

Text © 2000 Declan Carville

Book Design © 2000 Bernard O'Donnell

Illustrations © 2000 Brendan Ellis

A CIP catalogue record of this book is available from the British Library.

Printed in Belgium by Proost NV. Turnhout.

ISBN 0-9538222-0-6

1 2 3 4 5 6 7 8 9 10

# a day to remember at the Giant's Causeway

Declan Carville

illustrated by Brendan Ellis

book design by Bernard O' Donnell

Conor was tired. Very tired. In fact, he didn't want to move. "I want to stay here. Please. Just for a while..."

Murphy, his Red Setter, had other ideas.

"Get a move on Conor," he said, losing patience "It's late. Time is moving on."

"But all I want is a few more minutes. Please Murphy," replied the young boy lowering his head, "I'm always looking after you. Let me rest here. Please... just a little longer..."

Murphy sighed. It was true. Conor was his favourite, treated him better than anyone else in the family, like another human being. But now their friendship was being tested to the limit. As he watched his weary master the Setter felt the spray from the waves on his face. He had no choice. This time he had to take charge.

"I'll make a deal with you," said Murphy. "Walk to that last stone you can see ahead and I'll carry you on my back the rest of the way. But we must hurry - we've got to reach the grass before the sun goes down."

Conor raised his tired head and looked into the distance.

"In a minute..." the boy replied.

"Now!" demanded Murphy, surprised by the sharpness in his voice. "Now Conor," he pleaded "we have no time to lose..."

Out of nowhere a huge wave hit a nearby rock, soaking everything around. Conor jumped, startled by the force of the water but by the time he had managed to clear his eyes Murphy was already racing back from the waters edge, checking how much longer they had.

"Look," shouted Murphy above the shriek of the birds, "even the seagulls are warning us. If we move quickly we can rest in the caves near their nests. Please Conor, we must hurry." The Setter's tail now took on a frantic pace.

"I'm soaking," complained Conor, rising to his feet. "Do you promise... once we get to the stones..."

"Yes, yes," replied Murphy. "Now get a move on."

As the young boy began to move Murphy started to remember just how long a day it had been. It all seemed so far away. They had tired themselves out earlier on the beach, running in and out of the water, but now these threatening waves were advancing closer by the minute. And Conor was very small. They had to move quickly.

"These rocks are soaking. And slippy. I'm too tired..." complained Conor lowering himself to his knees for a better grip.

"You're doing fine," said Murphy. "Look at that crab. He's in a rush as well!" he added, trying to keep up the young lad's spirits.

"Aaaaaggggh!" cried Conor, rubbing the spray from his eyes, "I'm soaked."

There was another rush of waves, this time much closer, and the young boy had stopped again. He turned to Murphy to look for pity but his cry for help was not to be answered. Conor could scarcely believe the untidy sight in front of him. The Setter looked so different. The familiar shine of his coat had gone and was replaced by a tangled mess, his legs like sticks as the fur clung to his shivering body. Conor felt himself blush with shame.

"You've got seaweed Murphy," he murmured, "all around your legs."

"It doesn't matter," replied the Setter gazing ahead at the rocks. "I'm going to see how much further we have to go. I'll be back in a minute... Keep on the move. And be careful."

"But Murphy..." cried Conor as his friend set off into the distance.

Sitting on the rocks, Conor sat gazing out to sea. It had got a lot darker, he thought to himself, much darker than this afternoon. And the waves... the water was everywhere. For the first time he began to feel frightened. He turned back to face the climb but suddenly felt very alone.

"Murphy!... Murphy!..." he cried looking back up towards the rocks. "Where are you? Murphy!" he shouted, hearing the fear rise in his own voice.

Another wave broke, this time completely covering him. As he clung onto the slippery stones Conor felt something race over his hand. He screamed, but clearing his eyes he saw the Setter approach in the fading light.

"Murphy! Where were you? You left me here..." cried Conor, almost sobbing, but managing to hold back any tears. He could cry if he wasn't allowed to bring a football with them to the park or if he was scolded for not eating up like the others at meal times back home. But out here, surrounded by the threatening water under this darkening sky, crying just seemed out of the question.

"It's not too far," said Murphy, now back at his side. "If we keep moving we should be OK," he added, still looking into the distance.

"Can you carry me now?" begged Conor, holding out his arm.

"Not yet!" snapped Murphy. "We've still a bit of a climb. Keep moving."

This time Conor was close to tears.

"I'm so tired Murphy... Please..."

"I'm tired too, Conor," replied the Setter in a kinder voice, "but I'll walk beside you. That way we'll keep up with each other. Now come on. You're doing fine..." He knew the boy was exhausted.

At that moment, from out of nowhere, came more water. In a split second Murphy was gone.

"Murphy! Murphy!" cried Conor holding onto the rocks.

Knocked off his feet by the force of a wave, the Setter had been thrown sideways. As the air cleared Conor could see his friend struggling on the stones at a lower level.

"Murphy! Are you alright?" screamed Conor holding on as tight as he could. "Are you OK? Can you get back up here?"

He tried hard to hear the Setter's reply. Murphy was struggling to keep a grip on the stones which were fast becoming hidden beneath a bed of white foam from the sea. Waves seemed to be breaking all around.

"Murphy!" repeated Conor, "Murphy!"

"I'm OK!" shouted the Setter above the rush of the water. He had managed to get back up on all fours, for he knew it was up to him to lead the way. "Keep moving forward," he shouted. "We must get away from the waves. Keep moving!"

Conor couldn't believe what was happening. He wanted to wait for the Setter but even he knew now that he had to keep moving. He turned around to face the rocks once more and, as the spray trickled down his face, he began to climb.

The boy's progress was slow as the waves seemed to cover everything in sight. At one stage he raised his head and noticed a gull which had settled a few stones in front of him, its head darting about in different directions. The sight of the bird raised his spirits. 'He wouldn't be standing there if it was dangerous,' thought Conor to himself, 'we must be getting closer.' But within minutes the gull had flown off, joining the others circling overhead.

Looking down he could see Murphy below him. The Setter appeared to have hurt his leg but was still moving forward. As Murphy continued to climb upwards, Conor crawled downwards, now on all fours, over the maze of stones. The seaweed now clung like bandages around his own legs.

"Murphy! Murphy! Over here!" he shouted as they approached each other. "I'm so glad..." he continued, delighted to be reunited once again.

"Right sir," said Murphy, nearing his side, "on you get. We're not beaten yet..."

They had barely began to move forward when almost immediately darkness fell all around them, causing Conor to nearly lose his balance.

"Are you holding on tight Conor? Make sure you are holding on tight. We're not in the back garden now you know," said Murphy in a firm voice.

"Yes I'm holding on tight." said Conor. "But why is it so dark? So suddenly. I can't see a thing." He was starting to shout now. The darkness made him feel Murphy was further away than ever. "Do you think it's Finn MacCool, Murphy, do you? Daddy said he could come back. Is it him Murphy?" the young boy asked anxiously.

"It's not Finn MacCool," replied Murphy, stepping forward carefully.

"I knew it. I bet it's him," repeated Conor, the fear rising again in his voice. "He's come back Murphy! What are we going to do?"

"It's not Finn MacCool," repeated Murphy, trying to stay calm. "The sun has gone down. Or behind a cloud. Either way I'm not looking back to find out. Not now."

"Finn MacCool," Conor murmured to himself. "He's massive..."

"Hold on," interrupted Murphy, "we're on our way!"

With all the strength he had, Murphy started to move. It was hopeless trying to follow a path. Every stone looked the same, and there were thousands of them. The force of the water was fierce but at least the weight on his back prevented his legs from slipping any further. He knew his friends the seagulls would guide them.

Conor meanwhile had buried his head in the Setter's side. He was too frightened to look ahead. The air was filled with the cry of birds and the waves breaking all around them.

They seemed to climb forever, but suddenly Murphy came to an abrupt halt. What had happened? Conor felt hands...and arms...

"Finn MacCool! Aaaaagh! Get off me!!!" he shouted.

Conor jumped and was dazzled by a light.

"Up! Now!" said a stern voice.

The young boy struggled, trying to free his body from the grip.

"Leave me alone!" exclaimed Conor, "Let me go! Murphy! Help me!"

"Up!" the voice shouted back.

"Finn MacCool!" cried Conor, arms breaking loose in all directions, "you big bully!"

But wait a minute... He knew that voice.

Conor sat upright and looked around. Where was he? He felt in a daze. Somebody was shouting. But what was going on? Wasn't that his Mum's voice? Where's Finn...?

"You're blocking the way Conor," said his mother, losing patience. "Please. Get a move on. It's been a long day for all of us," she said, disappearing around the top of the stairs.

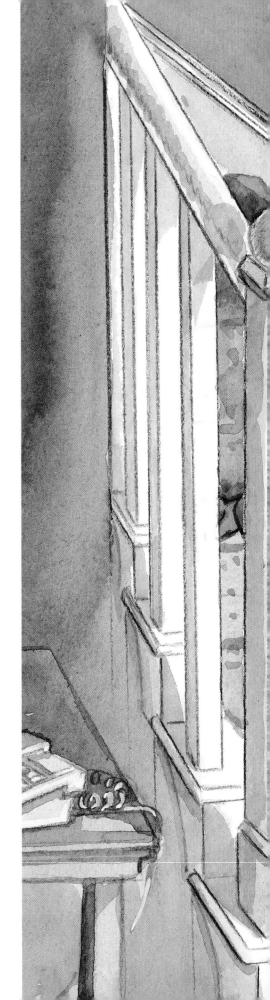

Conor couldn't move. He caught sight of his Dad coming through the front door, the picnic basket under his arm.

"Up the stairs Conor," he said, without raising his head. "Do as your mother tells you."

Conor sat on, trying to take it all in.

"Conor!" shouted his mother from the bedroom, "I'll not tell you again!"

At that, Murphy, the family dog, pushed past him on the staircase, causing him to nearly fall over.

He was sure the dog was wet.